Kitty's Magic

Scout the School Cat

Kitty's Magic

Scout the School Cat

Ella Moonheart

illustrated by Dave Williams

BLOOMSBURY
CHILDREN'S BOOKS
NEW YORK LONDON OXFORD NEW DELHI SYDNEY

BLOOMSBURY CHILDREN'S BOOKS
Bloomsbury Publishing Inc., part of Bloomsbury Publishing Plc
1385 Broadway, New York, NY 10018

BLOOMSBURY, BLOOMSBURY CHILDREN'S BOOKS, and the Diana logo
are trademarks of Bloomsbury Publishing Plc

First published in the United States of America in September 2020
by Bloomsbury Children's Books
www.bloomsbury.com

Bloomsbury books may be purchased for business or promotional use. For information on bulk
purchases please contact Macmillan Corporate and Premium Sales Department at
specialmarkets@macmillan.com

Library of Congress Cataloging-in-Publication Data
Names: Moonheart, Ella, author.
Title: Scout the school cat / by Ella Moonheart.
Description: New York : Bloomsbury, 2020. | Series: Kitty's magic ; 7 |
Summary: As the new school year starts and many students worry about
making friends, Kitty Kimura, a human girl who can transform into a cat,
tries to help an unhappy kindergartner and find a missing kitten.
Identifiers: LCCN 2020021995 (print) | LCCN 2020021996 (e-book)
ISBN 978-1-5476-0491-3 (paperback) • ISBN 978-1-5476-0492-0 (hardcover)
ISBN 978-1-5476-0493-7 (v. 7 ; e-book)
Subjects: CYAC: Cats—Fiction. | Magic—Fiction. | Shapeshifting—Fiction. | Friendship—Fiction. |
First day of school—Fiction. | Schools—Fiction. | Japanese Americans—Fiction.
Classification: LCC PZ7.1.M653 Sc 2020 (print) | LCC PZ7.1.M653 (e-book) | DDC [Fic]—dc23
LC record available at https://lccn.loc.gov/2020021995
LC e-book record available at https://lccn.loc.gov/2020021996

Printed and bound in the U.S.A. by Berryville Graphics Inc., Berryville, Virginia
2 4 6 8 10 9 7 5 3 1 (paperback)
2 4 6 8 10 9 7 5 3 1 (hardcover)

All papers used by Bloomsbury Publishing Plc are natural, recyclable products
made from wood grown in well-managed forests. The manufacturing processes
conform to the environmental regulations of the country of origin.

To find out more about our authors and books visit www.bloomsbury.com
and sign up for our newsletters.

Chapter 1

"Ready to go, Kitty?" asked Grandma.

"Ready!" replied Kitty Kimura, picking up her bag and taking a deep breath. "First day of school, here I come!"

"Let me take a photo of you before we set off. Smile!" said Grandma, snapping a picture on her phone. "I promised your parents I would send them one. They're going to be so proud of you!"

Kitty and Grandma left their house and walked down the street together, holding hands. Kitty's mom and dad were in Japan this week, looking for new things to sell in their special Japanese shop. Kitty missed them, but she was glad Grandma was taking her to school today. As they reached the gates, Kitty held Grandma's hand a little tighter, and stared at the ground.

"What's wrong, Kitty? I thought you were excited for your first day," said Grandma, looking worried.

"I am. But . . . well, it's just that I'm not going to be in the same class as

Jenny and Evie," she explained. "They're my best friends in the whole world! What if I don't see them anymore? And what if I don't make any new friends this year?"

"Oh, Kitty-cat. Don't worry," said Grandma gently, giving her a hug. "You will still see Jenny and Evie all the time. And you'll make lots of new friends, I promise. All you have to do is be yourself. Show your new class what makes Kitty Kimura special!" Her brown eyes twinkled, and she tapped the pretty necklace that Kitty was wearing. On the silver charm was a picture of a cat, along with some tiny words. "Although, maybe don't show them *everything* . . ."

Kitty couldn't help smiling. There was something *very* special about Kitty, but it was a big secret. When she said the magical words on her necklace, she turned into a cat! She could twitch her whiskers, swish her tail, and run along the tops of fences on her four padded paws. She could even talk to other cats.

Grandma was the only other person in the world who knew the secret, because she shared the same amazing gift. No one else could ever find out, though, not even Mom and Dad, or the magic would be broken.

Kitty stepped through the gates and looked at the school playground, with the school building ahead of her.

It looked bigger than she'd remembered it.

"There you are!"

Kitty heard footsteps behind her, and turned around. "Jenny! Evie!" she cried, waving as her best friends ran over.

"We've been looking all over for you!" said Jenny, giving her a big hug. "We thought, seeing as we're not in the same class as you this year . . ."

"We should all walk into school together!" finished Evie, grinning.

"We know you'll make lots of friends in your new class," Jenny said, "but the three of us are still going to hang out, right?"

"Definitely!" replied Kitty, beaming at her friends.

"You see?" whispered Grandma, kissing Kitty on her forehead. "You'll do great, Kitty."

The bell rang, and everyone started running toward the school building, shouting goodbye to their parents and grandparents. As Kitty passed a row of rosebushes on the edge of the playground, a movement caught her eye. She paused, seeing a pair of bright blue eyes and a small black nose. It was a tiny kitten, hiding behind the leaves. The kitten's coat was covered in black and brown splotches. Kitty knew that meant she was a tortoiseshell—because her markings looked a little bit like the shell of a tortoise. She wore a pretty blue collar to match her eyes.

What's a kitten doing all alone in the school playground? wondered Kitty.

She took a step toward the rosebushes, but the kitten gave a nervous squeal and darted away. Kitty was about to follow, but Evie was calling her.

"Kitty! Come on! If we're late on our first day, we'll get in trouble!"

Kitty knew she was right, so together they ran inside and found their new classrooms. Kitty was relieved to see that hers was right next door to Jenny and Evie's.

"Good luck!" called Jenny and Evie, waving as they walked inside.

Kitty suddenly felt nervous again. She peeped inside her own classroom, and saw rows of brightly colored desks and chairs, a cozy reading area with shelves full of books, and lots of animal posters decorating the walls. It definitely *looked* fun.

"Come inside! I'm Ms. Babbitt," said a woman with a kind smile, spotting Kitty at the door. She had very short blond hair and dangly silver earrings.

"Welcome to my class! Why don't you take this seat right here?"

Kitty put her school bag under her new desk and waved shyly at the girl sitting next to her. "Er, hi," she said. "I'm Kitty."

"My name's Mia," replied the girl, smiling. She had curly black hair, lots of freckles, and glasses with bright orange frames. "Oh, I love your necklace! Is that a cat? Cats are my favorite animal!"

"Mine too!" replied Kitty, reaching for her necklace. She wished she could tell Mia all about her magic secret, because she was sure Mia would want to be friends with her then. But she knew that wasn't allowed. *Just be yourself,* she thought, remembering Grandma's advice. "I don't have my own cat, though," she explained. "Do you?"

"Yes! I'll show you a picture," said Mia excitedly. She opened her pencil case and pulled out a photograph. "That's me, that's my little brother Nico, and that's our cat. Isn't he gorgeous?"

Kitty managed not to gasp out loud. She *knew* this cat! It was Tiger. He was the leader of the Cat Council, a group of cats who met whenever any cat in town had a problem or needed help.

She remembered Tiger telling her about his owner. "She's the sweetest little girl in the world!" he had purred. "She always makes sure I have lots of treats, and she brushes my fur really gently, so that I don't get knots or tangles. And she's always ready to play, the second she gets home from school. I'm one lucky cat!"

Kitty realized that all this time, Tiger had been talking about Mia—and now, Mia and Kitty were sitting together at school! *Now I'm the lucky one,* she thought happily. She could already tell that she and Mia were going to be friends. After all, they had something very important in common. Cats!

At the front of the classroom, Ms. Babbitt clapped her hands together. "Hello, everyone!" she called. "Now that you've all found your seats, I want to make a special announcement. I know some of you might be feeling a little nervous about starting this new school year. That's very normal, so don't worry. This week, we're going to spend lots of time getting to know each other."

Kitty and Mia glanced at one another and grinned.

"Starting school can be even harder

when it's your very first time," Ms. Babbitt continued. "Do any of you remember starting in kindergarten?"

Around the classroom, lots of heads nodded. "It was really scary," called a boy with curly black hair.

Ms. Babbitt smiled. "Right! Well, we have a brand-new kindergarten class starting at school today, and I'd like some volunteers to help them settle in. You will each be paired with a buddy from the kindergarten class. A few times a week, you'll meet up with your buddy and talk to them about starting school. You'll be someone they can talk to if they have any worries or questions."

It sounds a little bit like Cat Council, but for children instead of cats! thought Kitty, hiding a smile. She raised her hand. "I'd like to help," she said.

"So would I!" added Mia.

"Excellent," said Ms. Babbitt, as several more hands went into the air. "You'll all meet your kindergarten buddies soon!"

When the final bell rang that afternoon, Kitty and Mia walked outside together. A big group of people were waiting at the gates, waving. "There's my dad," Mia said, pointing at a tall man with curly hair just like hers. "I'd better go. Tiger will be missing me. I always give him a huge hug as soon as I get home. See you tomorrow, Kitty!"

"Bye!" called Kitty, waving as Mia

rushed off. She spotted Grandma and ran over.

"Kitty! How was your first day?" Grandma asked, opening her arms for a hug.

"It was great!" exclaimed Kitty. "I like my teacher a lot. And I'm sitting next to a really nice girl. She loves cats too!"

"That's wonderful, Kitty-cat," replied Grandma, smiling. "I'm proud of you."

Kitty skipped all the way home. She had made it through her first day of school *and* she had made a new friend— she couldn't wait to go back tomorrow!

Chapter 2

On Friday afternoon, Ms. Babbitt announced it was time for the volunteers to meet their kindergarten buddies. She led Kitty, Mia, and the other students down the hall. A friendly-looking man popped his head out from one of the doorways just as they reached it.

"Hi, everyone!" he said. "I'm Mr. Rolland. Come inside."

Everyone went into the classroom, which was very noisy. Kitty giggled as Mia nudged her and whispered, "They don't look like they need much help settling in, do they?" Mia was right— the kindergartners looked excited, shouting and laughing and bouncing on their chairs.

"Let's see," said Mr. Rolland, picking up a piece of paper. "Mia? Your buddy is Charlotte, sitting over there."

A tiny kindergartner with long braids and a bunny T-shirt stood up so quickly, she almost knocked over her chair. "Woops, careful!" laughed Mia.

Mr. Rolland read out the names of Kitty's classmates, and one by one, they went to sit with their buddies. Soon the room was full of chatter and laughter. Finally, Mr. Rolland reached the end of his list. "So you must be Kitty," he said, smiling at her. "Your buddy is Lila. Lila's sitting in the far corner, by the window."

Kitty looked where Mr. Rolland was pointing, expecting to see another excited face. Instead, she saw a little girl sitting by herself, staring sadly out of the window. Her arms were wrapped around her legs, and her chin rested on her knees.

Mr. Rolland bent down to whisper to Kitty. "Lila might need some extra help from you," he explained quietly. "She's finding it a bit tougher than the other children in my class to settle in."

Suddenly, Kitty felt really nervous.

Lila looked like she didn't want to talk to anyone! Mr. Rolland went on, "When I asked Ms. Babbitt who she thought would be the best buddy for Lila, she said your name right away."

"Really?" asked Kitty, surprised.

"Really! Ms. Babbitt thinks you're one of the friendliest, most helpful kids in her class."

Kitty walked over to Lila, feeling a little bit more confident. "Hello, Lila, I'm Kitty," she said, in a gentle voice. "I've just started in Ms. Babbitt's class, and I'm your new buddy."

Lila didn't even look up. Kitty decided to keep trying. "Do you like school so far?" she asked.

Lila shook her head.

"Why not?" asked Kitty. "Mr. Rolland seems really nice."

Lila glanced at her. "He is nice," she admitted in a small, sad voice. "But I don't have any friends here. I don't have anyone to talk to or to play with."

"Well, I'm your friend now!" Kitty told her. "And you can talk to me or play with me whenever you like. And I

bet lots of your classmates would like to be friends with you."

"I already have a best friend," Lila explained, looking gloomily at the floor. "But she's not here. And it feels really strange without her."

"Oh!" said Kitty. "That's exactly what happened to me this year, Lila! My two best friends are in a different class from me, too. So I know how you feel. But just because you're not in the same class doesn't mean you can't still be best friends, you know?"

But Lila didn't look very sure. And the more Kitty tried to chat to her buddy about her problem, the quieter Lila became.

Finally, Mr. Rolland clapped his

hands. "It's almost home time. Class, let's all say a big thank you to our new friends for visiting us today," he called.

Kitty thought Lila looked sadder than ever when she murmured a small "thank you."

"Don't worry. I promise it will get better," she told the little girl. "You'll see."

Mia couldn't wait to tell Kitty all about her own buddy. "Charlotte is really funny!" she said as they walked back to their classroom together. "She loves rabbits and soccer. What was your buddy like?"

Kitty sighed and explained her conversation with Lila.

"Poor Lila!" said Mia, frowning. "What are you going to do?"

Kitty shook her head. "I don't know, but I've got to help her. Maybe I'll ask my grandma what she thinks. She's good at helping people."

Once Kitty and Mia had collected their backpacks, they went into the playground to wait for Grandma and Mia's dad. Jenny and Evie were waiting for their parents too. "Hi, Kitty!" they called.

"Hi!" replied Kitty, smiling. "Mia, these are my best friends, Jenny and Evie. And this is Mia—we sit next to each other in class."

"You and Kitty are soooo lucky. Everyone says Ms. Babbitt is the nicest

teacher," Evie said to Mia. "Ms. Cortez is funny, but she's given us so much homework already."

Jenny nodded and pulled a face. "And I just wanted to spend the weekend playing with Misty!" she groaned. "I've missed her so much all week!"

"Misty is Jenny's cat," Kitty explained to Mia.

"I love cats!" said Mia excitedly. "I have a cat too."

"Ooh, we all love cats!" said Evie. "What's yours called?"

"Tiger. He's a big tabby tomcat," said Mia.

"I have two cats, Coco and Ruby. Ruby's just a kitten, and she's so, so cute," Evie said. "Hey, why don't you come over to my house tomorrow, and then you can meet them both, Mia? Jenny and Kitty are already coming over to hang out."

"Oh!" Mia blushed, but looked very pleased. "I'd love to. But I need to ask my dad. Hold on!"

Kitty watched as Mia rushed over to her dad, who had just arrived at the school gates. They spoke for a moment, then Mia turned round and nodded eagerly. "Dad says it's okay!" she called.

Kitty had a warm, happy feeling in her tummy. At the start of the week, she had been so worried that she wouldn't have any friends at school. Now, the four of them were going to spend tomorrow together!

This first week at school had almost been perfect—apart from Lila. Kitty thought again about the little girl, and her problem. *She misses her best friend,* Kitty remembered. *Next time I see her, I'll tell her that just because you make a new friend, it doesn't mean you have to lose your old ones!*

When Grandma arrived to collect Kitty, she was still thinking about Lila. "You look lost in thought!" chuckled Grandma, bending down to give her a hug.

Grandma listened, looking very thoughtful, as Kitty told her all about Lila.

"I really want to help her!" she finished.

"You will," Grandma told her. "You always do, Kitty. Just think about how many cats you have helped."

Grandma was right. Since Kitty had discovered her special gift, she had found lots of ways to help the cats in town. In fact, the Cat Council had decided to give Kitty a very important job: she was the Guardian of the Cat Council. That meant she used all her human knowledge to try to solve the most tricky cat problems.

That gave Kitty an idea. Lila had a *human* problem—so maybe Kitty could use her *cat* knowledge to solve it? She just didn't know how yet . . .

As Grandma and Kitty left the school playground, Kitty was still deep in thought—until something caught her eye. She gasped and pointed to a nearby oak tree. At the bottom of the trunk, a small triangle had been scratched into the bark.

"Grandma, the symbol!" she said. "Someone wants to call a meeting of the Cat Council!"

Chapter 3

After dinner that night, Kitty helped Grandma wash the dishes. They couldn't leave for the Cat Council meeting until it was dark, since people might notice all the cats in town heading to their meeting place. Kitty fidgeted impatiently until, finally, Grandma nodded. "It's time!" she said.

Kitty felt a shiver of excitement run

through her. She stood next to Grandma, and they both touched the silver cat necklaces they wore. Grandma's was just like Kitty's. "Let's say the words together," Grandma said. "Ready?"

"Ready!"

"*Human hands to kitten paws,*
Human fingers, kitten claws."

Kitty closed her eyes and waited for the magic to begin. First, she felt the tiniest tingle in her nose. It spread to her ears, then her neck, and through her shoulders and arms to her fingertips. It was like being filled up with shooting sparkles!

When the tingling sensation began to fade, she opened her eyes. Where Grandma had stood a moment ago, there was now a black cat with white markings—markings that looked just like the white streak in Grandma's black hair. Because this was Grandma—in her cat form!

And when Kitty looked down, she saw two small, furry black paws. Then she heard a happy rumbling sound. It was coming from deep inside her own throat. Kitty was purring because she, too, had turned into a cat!

"Come on!" meowed Grandma. She sprang onto the kitchen table, landing lightly on her paws before bounding up to the windowsill and out of the open kitchen window.

Kitty followed, enjoying the feeling of the air whooshing through her fur and whiskers. No matter how many times she turned into a cat, she never got used to how fast she could run, or how high she could jump. The world always felt bigger and more full of things to explore. She could squeeze through the tiniest gap in a garden fence and trot along the top of the highest walls without ever losing her balance. Flicking back her ears, she could even hear the tiny insects crunching through leaves and spiders spinning their delicate webs.

She and Grandma ran out of their yard and through the streets, their black tails swishing. It was dark now, but Kitty and Grandma didn't even need the streetlights, because their cat eyes could see perfectly, even at night.

As they turned a corner, Kitty's nose twitched. She could smell something coming—another cat! And she knew this cat's smell very well. Her best cat friend, Misty!

Sure enough, a silky gray kitten with darker gray stripes bounded along the street toward them. "Hi, Kitty!" called

Misty, trotting up to bump heads with Kitty. This was the special, friendly way for cats to say hello. "Hello, Suki," she added to Grandma. Suki was Grandma's name. "Do you know what the meeting is about?"

"Not yet!" replied Kitty. "Let's go find out. I hope we can help, whatever it is!"

Soon they were at the woods where the Cat Council always met. Kitty, Grandma, and Misty ran through the trees to a clearing where lots of cats were sitting in a circle, and more were padding in from every direction to join them. Kitty always loved seeing so many cats in one place! She meowed hello to an elegant white cat named Emerald and two excited twin kittens called Frost and Snowdrop. Then she spotted a big tomcat. This was Tiger—Mia's cat!

"Guess what, Tiger!" said Kitty, sitting down next to him. "I met your owner Mia at school this week. She's so nice! We're in the same class, and we're even sitting next to each other."

Tiger purred happily. "I know, Kitty. Every day when she gets home from school, Mia rushes straight inside to give me a treat and tell me all about her day at school—and she talks about you more than anything else!"

"Really?" asked Kitty.

"Really!" meowed Tiger, chuckling. "She was a little nervous about starting in her new class, but once she met you, she decided she was going to enjoy it. Now, I think we'd better start the meeting, Kitty—everyone seems to be here!"

Kitty looked around. The clearing was full of cats, some of them rubbing heads to say hello, and some of them slinking past one another to find a place to sit down, their collars glinting in the moonlight. There was a loud, low rumbling noise, which Kitty realized was the sound of lots of cats purring together.

Tiger called the meeting to attention. "Thank you for coming, everybody!" he meowed, nodding around the circle. "Let's start by saying the Meow Vow together, please!"

The cats all went quiet for a moment, before chanting the special, serious words they all said at the start of every Cat Council meeting.

"*We promise now,*
This solemn vow,
To help somehow,
When you meow."

"Excellent," Tiger said, purring as the vow ended. "Now, let's find out why we're all here! Who called this meeting, please?"

A small white cat with black smudges stood up and stepped into the middle of the circle. Kitty recognized Sooty, who lived just a few streets away from her. She had thrown a surprise birthday party for Sooty not long ago, and they had been friends ever since. "Sooty, could you tell us what the problem is?" she asked encouragingly.

Sooty nodded. "I wanted to ask for your help because I'm very worried about a new kitten in town," she explained.

"Oh dear. A kitten in trouble!" meowed Emerald, looking concerned.

"Who is this kitten, Sooty?" asked Suki.

"Her name is Scout," explained Sooty. "She and her family moved into the house opposite mine over the summer. She's quite shy and quiet, so we don't talk much, but I used to see her every morning, exploring in her yard. She loves playing with a little red ball and chasing bees."

"So why do you need our help?" asked Evie's gray cat, Coco, looking puzzled. "Scout sounds like a happy little kitten to me, even if she is a bit shy!"

"Well, she *was*," agreed Sooty. "But I haven't seen her for a few days. Every morning this week, I've checked her yard, and she's still not back in her usual spot. I think . . ." Sooty looked very upset now. "I think poor Scout might be lost!"

There was a worried murmur around the clearing. Tiger was nodding gravely. "I'm afraid you might be right, Sooty," he said. "If this kitten hasn't lived in our town for very long, she won't know her way around yet. If she wandered away from her street by accident, perhaps she can't find her way back."

"How awful!" meowed Misty.

Kitty thought so too. A tiny little kitten, lost and alone, and probably feeling very frightened by now! She and the Cat Council *had* to help.

"Sooty, when was the last time you saw Scout?" she asked.

"I saw her on Monday morning," Sooty

explained. "I remember because my human, Sophie, was getting ready for her first day of school, and her dad was taking a picture just as she left. I glanced out of the window and saw Scout then."

"That's really helpful," Kitty told her. "Can you describe what Scout looks like?"

Sooty thought for a moment. "She has tortoiseshell fur, a tiny black nose, and big blue eyes."

"Think hard, everyone," Suki told the cats around the circle. "Have any of you seen a kitten matching that description since Monday morning? If you have, that might give us a clue to where Scout is now."

The clearing fell silent as the cats

tried to remember—and so did Kitty. *Tortoiseshell fur, black nose, blue eyes*, she thought. *Why does that seem so familiar?*

And then she realized. "*I've* seen a kitten like that!" she cried.

The other cats meowed in excitement. "What? When, Kitty?" asked Suki.

"On Monday, in the school playground! It was just after you dropped me off," Kitty told her. "I ran toward school when the bell rang, with Evie and Jenny, and I saw something moving in the rosebushes. It was a tiny tortoiseshell kitten. I wondered what she was doing there, but before I could get closer, she ran off." Suddenly she remembered something else.

"Sooty, does Scout wear a bright blue collar?"

"Yes!" meowed Sooty, nodding quickly. "The exact same shade of blue as her eyes."

"Then it must have been Scout I saw," Kitty replied.

"Monday . . . ," murmured Suki, looking very thoughtful.

"What is it?" Kitty asked her.

"You saw Scout on Monday morning," explained Suki. "Kitty, I think you might have been the last person to see Scout before she went missing!"

Chapter 4

A ripple of anxious whispers spread around the Cat Council.

"But what was Scout doing in the school playground?" Sooty asked. "That's a really long way from our street!"

"It's an especially long way for a little kitten," added Shadow.

"There are lots of garages and garden

sheds on the way. Scout might have been exploring and got trapped in one!" squealed a cat named Sparkle.

Emerald gasped. "There are plenty of busy roads to cross on the way there, too. I hope Scout hasn't been in an accident."

Kitty thought back to that morning at school. "Oh, I just wish I'd done something!" she meowed sadly. "I thought it was strange for a kitten to be alone in the school playground. So why didn't I catch her? It's all my fault that she's missing!"

There were loud meows from around the circle. "It's not your fault, Kitty!" Tiger told her firmly. "You know as well as anyone that kittens are very fast.

Even if you'd tried to catch her, she would have run off."

"And remember, Scout doesn't know that you're a special human who can turn into a cat!" Suki added. "She wouldn't have known she could trust you."

"Besides, we know you'll help get Scout back, Kitty!" Misty told her, purring encouragingly.

Kitty nuzzled her friend's head gratefully. She felt a little bit better— but secretly, she still thought that she could have helped Scout. She had just been so wrapped up in her worries about her first day at school!

"What do you think we should do?" asked Shadow.

All the cats looked at Kitty.

"Tomorrow, let's all split up into groups," she said. "We can each search a different part of town. That way, we can make sure we're not missing anywhere."

"That's a good idea," said Emerald, her white ears perking up. "Where shall I look, Kitty?"

"Could you, Frost, and Snowdrop search the park?" asked Kitty. "And Tiger, Misty, and Shadow, maybe you could cover the shops and the library."

"What about us?" meowed Coco. "Ruby and I want to help too."

"Why don't you look by the swimming pool? And Sooty and Sparkle, how about you take the school playground?"

"We'll make sure we check all the rosebushes, just in case Scout has gone back there!" said Sooty.

"We'll meet back here tomorrow night and tell the rest of the Council what we find," Kitty finished, once she'd paired each set of cats and given them a spot to search. "Hopefully, one of us will find a clue that will lead us to Scout.

Or, even better, one of us might find Scout herself!"

There was an enthusiastic purr around the clearing. Kitty watched as the cats sprang away and began running back home. Everyone was going to need lots of rest before the search began tomorrow!

The next morning, Kitty bounced out of bed. "Time to start looking for Scout!" she announced, bursting into the kitchen.

Grandma smiled. "How about some pancakes first, Kitty-cat?" she suggested, holding up a mixing bowl full of batter. "If we're going to search the whole town, we'll need energy!"

Kitty slid into her seat at the table. "I

was thinking," she told Grandma, "every cat in town is going to be looking for Scout today, and they'll be able to look in all the tiny nooks and crannies where a kitten might be. But there are also lots of places to look that a cat won't be able to get to very easily that a person can! So I think we should search in our human forms."

Grandma nodded thoughtfully as she flipped a pancake. "That's very true, Kitty. We can be more helpful searching as humans. We can also ask other people if they've seen a lost kitten. I could call the vet and ask if any kittens have been brought into the hospital this week."

"Yes, Grandma, that's a great idea!"

said Kitty. "Oh, wait—I've just thought of something else."

She jumped up from the table and rummaged in a drawer until she pulled out a pad of white paper and her colored pencils. While Grandma finished the pancakes, Kitty started to draw. Finally she held it up. "What do you think?"

Kitty had sketched Scout, using as many shades of brown, black, and white as she could to show the kitten's special tortoiseshell coat. With her brightest blue pencil, she had added Scout's eyes and matching collar, and at the top of the page, in rainbow letters, she had written: LOST! HAVE YOU SEEN THIS KITTEN?

"We can show it to people in town today," she explained to Grandma.

"Excellent, Kitty!" said Grandma, nodding. "You could start with Evie and Jenny, couldn't you?"

Kitty stared at Grandma. "I just remembered! I'm supposed to be hanging out with Evie, Jenny, and Mia today. How can I search for Scout?"

But even as she asked the question, Kitty realized . . . four pairs of eyes were much better than one! "I bet they'll want to help, too," she said. "Don't you think so?"

Grandma's eyes twinkled as she slid pancakes onto both plates. "I know so, Kitty."

* * *

Kitty rode her bicycle over to Evie's house as soon as she'd finished breakfast, with her picture of Scout rolled up carefully in her backpack. Jenny was already there, playing with Coco and Ruby in Evie's bedroom. The cats ran over to nuzzle Kitty with their noses, and when Evie and Jenny went to fetch drinks from the kitchen, she bent down and whispered, "Good luck searching today!"

Mia arrived soon after, smiling shyly as Evie opened the door. "Thanks for inviting me!" she said, flashing a wide grin at Kitty.

"No problem! What should we do first?" said Evie as they all clattered back up the stairs to her room.

sk if they had seen a small
ll kitten with blue eyes and a
r. Most people just shook
s, although an elderly lady
k glasses looked at Kitty's
ry carefully before deciding
n't help them, and a friendly
girl promised she'd look out
t.

bent down to check under cars,
od on tiptoes to peer over
Mia even climbed onto Jenny's
rs to look in the branches of the
ust in case Scout had scampered
unk and hadn't been able to get
They almost slipped a couple of
, and Kitty wished she could turn
a cat and leap up there with her

"Actually," Kitty said quickly, "I
wanted to ask you all for your help."
She pulled the drawing out of her
backpack and spread it flat.

"A lost kitten?" said Jenny, her eyes
wide. "Oh gosh, poor little thing!"

Kitty nodded. "I noticed her hiding
in a bush in the school playground this
week. She ran away before I could get
too close, but she looked like she might
be lost. I was thinking we could go
out and look for her."

"Definitely!" said Jenny. "Oh, I hope
we find her!"

"We should make copies of your
poster, Kitty," suggested Mia. "Maybe
we can stick them up around town."

"Good idea! Here, we can use my

coloring things," said Evie, pulling a box from underneath her bed. Quickly, the girls made their own sketches of Scout, adding Kitty's message at the top.

"Finished!" said Jenny, holding hers up.

"Me too!" said Mia. "Let's go out on our bikes; it'll be quicker that way!"

"I'll just go and ask my mom and dad," added Evie. She ran downstairs to the kitchen, calling for her parents. A minute later, she reappeared. "Mom says it's okay, as long as we all stay together. And we have to be back in time for lunch!"

Kitty grabbed her backpack and put the rolled-up posters inside it. Then

strong back legs and sharp claws. Some things were so much easier as a cat!

When they reached the shops in the middle of town, Kitty and Mia popped into the post office to ask if they could stick one of their posters in the window.

"Is that you, Kitty?"

Kitty turned to see a smiling lady in the line to mail a package. "Ms. Babbitt!" she said, recognizing her new teacher.

"It *is* you! And Mia too! How lovely to see you two spending time together outside school. What are you both up to this morning? You look very busy!"

Kitty explained that they were searching for a lost kitten, and showed Ms. Babbitt the poster. She studied it carefully. "I'll certainly keep an eye out," she promised the girls. "I'll make sure I let the other teachers at school know, too, as the kitten was last seen in the playground. I'm sure she'll turn up!" She looked thoughtfully at the poster again. "Funny that the town isn't covered in these! Perhaps the cat's owner just didn't have the bright idea to make a poster, unlike you girls."

Once they headed back outside, Evie was looking anxiously at her watch. "I'm really sorry, but I told my parents we'd only be out for a couple of hours," she explained. "They said to be back for lunch at one o'clock."

"That's okay. We'll ride back to your house and keep looking on the way," Jenny told her. "I can't believe we haven't spotted any sign of this kitten yet! It feels like we've looked everywhere!"

"I'm sorry it's taken the whole morning," Kitty said, looking at the others. "I really thought we could find her."

"We wanted to help!" said Evie.

"That's what friends are for, right?" added Jenny.

Kitty felt a rush of affection for her friends.

"And even though we didn't find the kitten, we've told lots of people about her, and shown them our posters," pointed out Mia. "Although . . ."

"What?" asked Kitty, as Mia frowned.

"It's just something Ms. Babbitt said," Mia explained. "It got me thinking. She said it was odd that the town wasn't covered in posters. Well, she's right, isn't she?"

"What do you mean?" asked Evie.

"If Scout really is a lost cat, wouldn't her owners be out searching for her?" said Mia. "And wouldn't they have put up posters all around town? But it feels like the only people looking for Scout are . . ."

"Us," finished Kitty, nodding.

Mia was right. Kitty couldn't believe she hadn't thought of it before. Why weren't Scout's owners out looking for their kitten? Was Scout really a lost kitten—or was something else going on?

Chapter 5

An owl hooted in the trees as Kitty and
Suki ran back to the clearing that night,
their ears pricked up and their tails
swishing.

Kitty had spent the rest of the day
searching for Scout, even after she'd
had to say goodbye to Evie, Jenny, and
Mia. She had had no luck. She was
keeping her paws crossed that another
cat would have better news.

But when the Cat Council was gathered in a circle, a quick scan of her fellow cats told Kitty that none of them had seen Scout either. Everyone looked disappointed, their heads hanging. As Tiger asked each cat to step forward and report what they had found, she heard the same story again and again. "Not a whisker!" said Coco, shaking her head sadly. "We sniffed every corner of our little patch so carefully, but we didn't find any smells that might lead us to Scout."

"We looked in the flowerbeds in the park. We were hoping we might find some kitten pawprints, but all we found was ladybugs and beetles," said Emerald.

"We did pick up Scout's scent in the

school playground, in the rosebushes where you saw her, Kitty," explained Sooty. "But we lost it just outside the school gates. There are just too many other smells there."

"So what happens now?" asked Frost worriedly. "We've run out of places to look!"

Kitty was very quiet, thinking hard. *Had* they run out of places to look—or was there one last place she just hadn't thought of yet? Suddenly she remembered what Mia and Ms. Babbitt had said earlier. They had thought it was strange that Scout's owners hadn't put up posters of her . . .

"It sounds like we should call it a night for now," meowed Tiger. "But we won't give up! Everyone, keep looking out for Scout. Call another meeting if you have news!"

The cats began padding out of the clearing, muttering sadly. As Kitty saw Sooty leaving, she had an idea. The cats had searched all over town, but there *was* one place they hadn't looked yet!

"Wait, Sooty!" she meowed, trotting up to the little white-and-black cat. "Can you show me where Scout lives? I want to have a closer look."

"Sure," said Sooty. "Follow me."

She led Kitty through the moonlit streets, darting around street corners and tiptoeing quietly past the front door of a particularly growly dog. Finally, Sooty stopped outside a house with a wading pool and a swing in the garden. All the curtains were drawn, and the house was quiet and dark. "It looks like they're all asleep," whispered Sooty. "Listen, Kitty, I need to get back to my own house. I sleep at the end of Sophie's bed, and if she wakes up in the night and I'm not there, she'll be worried."

"Okay, Sooty," replied Kitty, nodding. "I understand."

"Sorry I can't stay and help, but I hope you find a clue about where Scout might be! The cat flap is around the back," she added, pointing a paw.

Once Sooty had padded over the road to her own house, Kitty trotted around Scout's yard, looking for anything that might be a clue. The yard was full of plants and flowers and buzzing with fireflies and crickets. Scattered on the grass, she found lots of colorful bouncy balls and some squeaky toy birds covered in tiny kitten-size teeth marks. But there was no sign of the kitten herself.

Kitty glanced up at the house. *I've*

got to go inside! she told herself. *This is where Scout lives, so there's got to be a good clue here about where she might be! Everyone's asleep, so I'll just have to be really, really quiet.*

Kitty padded around the back of the house and found the cat flap. She took a deep breath, held out one paw, and pushed.

The cat flap didn't budge.

Puzzled, Kitty butted it with her forehead. Still, the cat flap didn't open. *What's going on?* she wondered.

Then, at the bottom of the cat flap, she noticed a small latch. The cat flap wasn't moving because it had been locked shut!

Kitty had never seen this before.

Why would anybody ever lock a cat flap? Was Scout's family trying to keep another cat *out* of their house?

Or, thought Kitty, *are they trying to keep Scout in?*

She looked back at the toys scattered around the garden. This seemed like a family who really loved their kitten— a kitten who really loved playing outside! So why would the family want to keep her locked inside?

At the corner of the yard was a tall tree. Kitty grabbed the trunk with her sharp claws and climbed up to the branches, her tail waving from side to side to help her balance. Once she was safely in the tree, she looked back at the house. Now that she was up high, she could see through the gaps in the curtains.

On the left, there was a large bedroom where two grown-ups in stripy pajamas were fast asleep in bed. Next to that was another, smaller bedroom, this one lit by a cozy-looking night-light shaped like a moon. Tucked up in bed was a small dark-haired girl, and curled up beside her was a tiny, furry tortoiseshell bundle.

Scout!

The little girl yawned, and as she did, Kitty caught sight of her face. To her surprise, she realized she knew her, too. It was Lila, her kindergarten buddy from school!

Kitty gasped—and as she did, the

kitten's tiny ears pricked up. She sat up, looked around, and meowed curiously. Then, with a wiggle, she leaped from the bed onto the windowsill, and poked her furry head out of the window, which was open a few inches.

Kitty walked toward the little kitten and perched at the end of the branch. "Hello!" she said softly. "My name's

Kitty. I'm so happy to meet you, Scout. I've been looking everywhere for you. All the cats at the Cat Council have!"

"What's the Cat Council?" asked Scout shyly.

Kitty quickly explained. "It was Sooty, the mostly white cat who lives across the road, who told us about you," she added. "She was so worried when you stopped going out to play in your garden."

"I didn't think any cats in this town even knew who I was!" meowed Scout in surprise. "I don't have any cat friends here, just my best friend Lila."

She nodded at the sleeping girl, and Kitty chuckled. "I know Lila!" she explained. "We go to school together." She thought back to her first meeting with Lila, and remembered Lila talking about her best friend. She had thought she meant a human best friend—when all this time, she'd been talking about her cat!

"How do you go to school with Lila?" meowed Scout. "You're a cat!" Her tiny black nose twitched suddenly, and she looked confused. "Although, you do smell a bit . . ."

"Human?" guessed Kitty. "I know! That's because I'm really a human girl, but I can change into a cat. That's a big secret, though."

Scout's big blue eyes grew even wider. "I've never heard of a girl who could turn into a cat before," she said. "Wow! I wish Lila could do that, so that she could spend the day with me instead of having to go to kindergarten."

"She really doesn't like it there, does she?" asked Kitty gently, glancing back at Lila asleep in her bed.

"All summer, she was so scared about starting kindergarten!" explained Scout. "She doesn't make new friends very easily, even though she's the sweetest girl in the world. So I decided to go with her, on her first morning. I crept out the cat flap and followed her there. I thought I could keep her company. Only when I got into the school playground, it was so busy and noisy! So I hid in the bushes."

"That's when I saw you!" realized Kitty.

"Then I ran back home again. But Lila's dad saw me crossing a big road, with lots of scary cars all beeping their horns at me! So he and Lila's mom decided I had to stay inside until I'm bigger, to keep me safe." Scout gave a sad little meow. "That's why the cat flap is locked. Now I can't even play with my toys in the yard anymore."

"So all this time, you haven't been lost," said Kitty. "You've been at home, locked inside!"

Scout nodded miserably. "I only wanted to help Lila," she said. "And with her being at school all day, I'm getting really lonely."

"Well, don't worry. I'm sure I can do something to—"

Just then, Lila gave another yawn and rolled onto her side, rubbing her eyes. "Scout?" she said sleepily. "Scout, what are you doing at the window?"

"Bye!" Kitty whispered. Then she leaped down the tree trunk and into the yard. As she left Scout's house and began running toward her own, she glanced up at the window one last time. She had found the missing kitten—but Scout still needed her help. And so did Lila!

Chapter 6

"Morning, Kitty!" called Mia, waving as she opened her front door. "Quick, come inside. I want you to meet Tiger!"

It was Monday morning, and Kitty and Mia had decided to walk to school together.

But Kitty had another, secret reason for coming to Mia's house. She wanted to give a message to Tiger. And Mia had just given her the perfect opportunity!

"Yes, please!" Kitty said, grinning as she stepped inside Mia's house.

"Here he is!" Mia said, scooping Tiger into her arms and rubbing her face against his tabby fur. "Isn't he the most gorgeous cat you've ever seen? Would you like to hold him?"

"I'd love to. Hi, Tiger!" said Kitty, holding out her arms for the tabby tom. She giggled as Tiger purred loudly.

"He likes you!" said Mia happily. "I'll just run and grab my bag."

As soon as Mia ran upstairs, Kitty whispered to Tiger, "I found Scout! She's okay—her family locked her inside their house because they were

worried about her running over a busy road. Tell the other cats, especially Sooty. I don't want them to be worried about her!"

Tiger meowed to let Kitty know he'd understood, and Kitty bent down to let him jump back onto the ground. Tiger leaped straight onto a table and out an open window. Kitty knew he would be heading off to find the other cats in town.

"Ready!" said Mia, coming downstairs with her bag. She held up a book for Kitty to see. "This was my favorite story in kindergarten. I thought I'd take it to read with my buddy Charlotte today!"

"That's a great idea," Kitty told her friend as they started walking to school.

"Do you know how you're going to help Lila yet?" asked Mia.

Kitty sighed and shook her head. Today, she, Mia, and the rest of their classmates would be seeing their kindergarten buddies for the second time. Kitty had been thinking hard about Lila—and Scout—but she still didn't have any good ideas. Scout couldn't come to school to keep Lila company, but Lila couldn't stay at home with Scout either!

"Don't worry," said Mia, putting her arm around Kitty. "You'll think of something, I know you will!"

Ms. Babbitt led Kitty and Mia to the kindergarten class straight after lunch that day. Kitty crossed her fingers as she walked into the room, hoping to see a big smile on Lila's face, but instead, Lila was still sitting alone, looking more miserable than ever. In fact, as Kitty walked over to her, she saw tears rolling down Lila's face. Kitty's heart sank.

"Lila! What's wrong?" she asked, kneeling down beside her buddy.

Lila sniffed and rubbed her eyes. "We're doing Show and Tell every Friday," she explained in a shaky voice. "And this week, it's my turn! Mr. Rolland says I've got to talk in front of the whole class, and I'm so nervous! And I don't have anything special to show anyway."

"Oh, Lila!" Kitty gave her buddy a hug. "Listen, it's always a little scary the first time you do Show and Tell, but I promise it's going to be okay! And I'll help you think of something to show."

As Kitty went to get Lila a tissue, her very first morning at school suddenly popped into her head. She remembered walking into the play-ground with Grandma, feeling worried about starting in her new class, and Grandma telling her to show everyone what made *her* special. When Kitty had got into the classroom, she and Mia had bonded straight away because they both loved cats. That was what made them special.

So what made Lila special?

It was the same thing, Kitty realized. Lila was special because of how much she loved cats. And not just any cat!

"Lila," said Kitty, handing her the tissue, "is it true that you have a kitten?"

Lila's head popped up straight away. "How do you know about Scout?" she asked.

Kitty shrugged. "Oh, er, I think I heard Mr. Rolland mention it. Scout, that's such a cute name! What's she like?"

Kitty had never seen Lila smile before, but now the little girl's face broke into a huge beam. "She's the best kitten ever!" she told Kitty. "She's three months old, and she's a tortoiseshell. Do you know what that means?"

Kitty nodded, smiling. "Yes, I do. I like cats too!"

"Do you?" gasped Lila. "Oh, I love cats! Especially Scout. Mom and Dad got her for me when we found out we had to move. She has this tiny little black nose, and eyes that are really bright blue, and little furry ears that I love tickling . . ."

Lila began chattering eagerly about

Scout. Across the room, Kitty saw Mr. Rolland give her a thumbs-up. For the first time, Lila seemed happy, and not shy at all.

If only the rest of the class could see this side of Lila, Kitty thought. She was sure Lila would fit right in at kindergarten then.

That's it!

A plan sprang into Kitty's head. *I'm going to need some help*, she thought. *But if this works, it could solve Lila's problem, and help Scout too . . .*

When Kitty knocked on Mia's door on Friday morning, she felt as though she had ten wriggly kittens in her tummy. She was nervous, impatient, and excited, all at the same time!

She smiled as Mia opened the door. "Show and Tell time! Let's go!"

"I can't wait!" Mia said, clapping her hands together. "Mr. Rolland knows your plan?"

"Yes, he loved the idea. So did Ms. Babbitt. And Lila's mom and dad said it was okay too!"

"Yes!" Mia held out her hand for a high five. "Let's just hope it works."

Show and Tell started at two o'clock, so at five to two, Ms. Babbitt gave permission for Kitty, Mia, and the other volunteers to go down the hall to the kindergarten class. "Good luck, girls!" she said, winking at them as they left their seats.

"Thanks!" said Kitty, smiling at her teacher.

Everyone in Lila's class was sitting in a big circle on the mat when Kitty and Mia got to the room. The other volunteers rushed to meet their buddies, but Lila was waiting at the door for Kitty. Her cheeks were very pink, and she was doing a little excited dance. "Mom said she'd be here at two!" she whispered, glancing up at the clock on the wall. "I hope she's not late!"

"She'll be here!" Kitty promised. "My grandma talked to her on the phone last night," she added, taking Lila back into the classroom.

Just then, there was a knock at the door, and a woman with round glasses and dark hair like Lila's popped her head into the classroom. "Hi, Lila!"

"Mom, you made it just in time!" said Lila, relieved.

"And you must be Kitty?" the woman asked.

"Yes!" Kitty rushed out into the hallway. She saw a large basket on the floor next to Lila's mom's feet. "Is that her?"

"That's her!" said Lila's mom. "I wish I could stay to watch, but I have to rush home, I'm afraid. I know she's in excellent hands, though. Lila said you loved cats, just like her."

"I do, more than anything!" Kitty said.

Lila's mom smiled. "I wanted to thank you for being such a thoughtful buddy to Lila. She's been talking about you all week."

When Lila's mom had left, Kitty lifted the lid of the basket and peered inside. Two big, blue eyes blinked nervously back at her.

"Hi, Scout! It's me, Kitty," she whispered, reaching inside the basket to stroke Scout's silky tortoiseshell fur. "Do you remember me?"

Scout purred and nuzzled her nose

against Kitty's hand. "Listen, Scout—Lila's just through that door," Kitty told her. "She's so excited you're here. Now, are you ready?"

Scout gave a soft meow, and gently, Kitty put the lid back on the basket and pushed open the classroom door.

The circle of children began chatting excitedly as Kitty walked in holding the basket, and handed it carefully to a giddy Lila. "Settle down, everyone!" called Mr. Rolland. "This is a very special Show and Tell, and I need everyone to stay nice and quiet, okay? Now, let's see what Lila has to show us!"

As Lila opened the basket and lifted out Scout, the room gasped. "A kitten!" squeaked a girl with brown hair.

"Wait a second! Isn't that the kitten we were searching for last week?" whispered Mia to Kitty.

"I think you might be right," she whispered back. "What a coincidence!"

"Is that *your* kitten, Lila?" asked a boy.

Lila nodded shyly. "Her name is Scout," she said, her voice very quiet.

Come on, Lila! thought Kitty, smiling at her buddy. *You can do this!*

Scout must have been thinking the same thing, because Kitty saw the kitten give Lila's hand a gentle lick with her tiny pink tongue. Lila giggled. "She's my best friend," she told the room proudly.

"What else can you tell us about Scout, Lila?" asked Mr. Rolland.

"Well, she loves treats," said Lila. "When I come home from school, I always get her a bowl of her favorite cat treats. Then my dad gets me one of his homemade chocolate brownies, and Scout and I sit and eat our treats together!"

"Yum!" said Mia's buddy Charlotte, laughing. "I have a pet rabbit at home, and my mom always makes us carrot sticks to nibble on together after school. Your dad's brownies sound much tastier, though!"

"They *are* really yummy!" said Lila.

"Oh wow, look at her tiny little teeth," said a boy, pointing at Scout. "They're so cute!"

"They're just her baby teeth,"

explained Lila. "Cats are just like people. When they get old enough, their baby teeth fall out, and they get adult teeth instead. I don't think they get to put their baby teeth under their pillow for the tooth fairy, though," she added.

The class laughed. "You're really funny, Lila," said the boy, grinning.

"Can I pet her, Lila? I have a cat at home, so I know how to do it," said another boy.

"Sure," said Lila. "Wow, I didn't know you had a cat too, Charlie."

"So do I!" called a few more children around the room.

Kitty smiled as Charlie reached out to gently pet Scout, and Scout began purring happily. Lila looked almost like she could start purring any second, too. Kitty had never seen her buddy look so happy.

"Hey, Lila, maybe you could come and meet my rabbit this weekend?" suggested Charlotte when it was her turn to stroke Scout.

"Oh, I'd love to. Thanks," said Lila, blushing. She caught Kitty's eye and gave her a huge smile.

Kitty beamed back. Her Show and Tell plan had worked. Lila had shown her class what made her special—and she'd made lots of new friends!

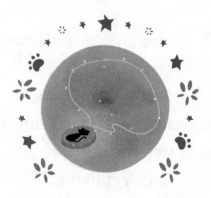

Chapter 7

Kitty and Lila walked out of school together a short while later, carrying Scout's basket between them. Scout was snuggled inside, purring. Lila was grinning proudly. It seemed like everyone in school was talking about her and her kitten.

"That was the best Show and Tell ever, Lila," one boy in her class called as he ran past her.

"Oh, thanks, Charlie!" said Lila happily.

"Don't forget about meeting Clive this weekend, Lila! That's my rabbit!" said Charlotte, waving.

"I can't wait!" replied Lila.

Grandma was waiting at the school gates to walk both Kitty and Lila home. "Well, I can tell from your faces that Show and Tell was a big success!" she said, chuckling. "Tell me all about it!"

"Everyone loved Scout!" said Lila excitedly. "And once I'd started telling everyone about Scout, everyone wanted to talk to me, too! I didn't know so many other kids in my class liked animals, especially cats. They're all so friendly, and it felt much easier with Scout there. And you, Kitty."

"Well done, Kitty-cat," Grandma whispered. "I'm very proud of you for helping out your new friend."

"I still have one more thing to do," Kitty whispered back. "Lila has lots of friends at school now, but I have to make sure that Scout isn't lonely while Lila's gone!"

When they reached Lila's house, Lila ran up the garden path. "Mom! Dad!" she shouted. "I had so much fun at school today!"

Lila's parents appeared at the door, smiling. "I'm very happy to hear that!" said Lila's mom. "So Show and Tell went well?"

Lila eagerly began telling them about her day, while Kitty and Grandma brought the basket to the door. Lila's mom thanked them. "You've been such a good buddy to Lila, Kitty," she told her. "And you've done such a great job of looking after Scout today, too! Was she any trouble on the way home?"

"Trouble?" said Kitty, surprised. "No, why?"

"Oh, that's good to hear! It's just that she ran away from home earlier this week. Lila's dad saw her running across a really busy road, and we were so worried about her. We've had to keep her inside all week. It's been really hard—she does love playing outdoors."

Now it was time for Kitty to put the

next part of her plan into action! "Scout was really well-behaved all day," she explained. "I think when she ran away, she might just have been following Lila to school. Cats are really smart, you know. They can tell when a human is feeling upset or nervous, like Lila was."

"That's very true," added Grandma.

"I didn't know that!" said Lila's mom, looking impressed. "Lila and Scout *are* very close."

"Now that Scout has been to school with Lila, and she's seen how happy Lila is there, I don't think she'll run away again," Kitty said. She crossed her fingers tightly. Had she said the right things?

Lila's mom looked thoughtful. "You

know, I think you may be right," she said. "We just wanted to keep her safe, but Scout has seemed so unhappy being cooped up in the house these last few days. Maybe we'll let her into the yard tomorrow and see how it goes."

"Great!" said Kitty, grinning.

She helped Lila open the basket and gently lift out Scout, who was meowing happily and trying to lick Kitty's hands. Kitty couldn't talk to Scout while Lila and her parents were here, but she knew what Scout was trying to say. She had heard what Lila's mom had just told Kitty. Scout was going to be allowed back outside—and she couldn't wait!

Kitty hugged Lila and scratched Scout's head, then set off back down the garden path with Grandma. "Bye, Kitty!" called Lila, waving. "Thanks for being the best buddy ever!"

"See you tomorrow, Lila!" said Kitty, smiling.

As she and Grandma turned the corner, Kitty grabbed a twig from the ground and knelt down to scratch a triangle in the trunk of a nearby tree. "Another Cat Council meeting?" said Grandma. "What for, Kitty? I thought you had solved Scout's problem!"

"There's just one more thing I need to ask the cats," explained Kitty mysteriously. "You'll see, Grandma!"

"Wait for us, Kitty!"

Kitty was halfway to school the next

morning when she heard footsteps behind her. She turned to see Mia, Jenny, and Evie rushing up the street.

"Hi, guys!" said Kitty.

"We were hoping we'd catch up with you!" said Jenny, panting. "Mia told us that the kitten we were looking for has been found."

"We couldn't believe it!" said Evie, grinning. "It's the best news!"

"Yes, she was right under our noses the whole time!" said Kitty, laughing.

"Well, I'm just glad that she's safe and happy," said Mia, smiling. "She's such a cute little kitten."

Just then, in a flash of black, gray, and ginger fur, three cats ran past them on the street. "Wow, they're in a hurry!"

joked Jenny. "I wonder what they're up to?"

Kitty smiled as the cats leaped over a fence, headed in the direction of Scout's house. At the Cat Council meeting last night, she had asked for volunteer buddies—cats who would keep Scout company during the day, while Lila was at school. Every single cat wanted to

volunteer! In fact, they were going to have to take turns. Otherwise, Kitty thought Lila's parents might wonder why their yard was suddenly full of cats.

Lila and Scout now had plenty of friends in their town, and Kitty felt lucky that she could be friends with them both. Plus, she had her *best* friends—three of them. Jenny, Evie, *and* Mia.

"Looks like they're having a race," she said, watching the cats disappear out of sight. "Come on, let's see who can get to school fastest! Ready, set, go!"

And Kitty Kimura and her best friends flew down the street together.

MEET

Kitty

Kitty is a little girl who can magically turn into a cat! She is the Guardian of the Cat Council.

Tiger

Tiger is a big, brave tabby tomcat. He is leader of the Cat Council.

Suki is Kitty's grandmother. She can magically turn into a cat too!

Suki

THE CATS

Misty

Misty is Kitty's best cat friend. She loves snoozing in the sunshine.

Sooty is a black and white cat. Her favorite food is sardines, and she doesn't like surprises.

Sooty

Scout

Scout is a little kitten who loves her owner, Lila! She also loves playing outdoors with her new cat friends.

FELINE FACTS

Here are some
fun facts about our
purrrfect animal friends
that you might like
to know...

1.

Except for kittens (who meow for their mothers), cats don't meow to communicate with each other, only with humans.

2.

The oldest recorded living cat was Crème Puff of Austin, Texas, who lived to be 38 years and 3 days old.

3.

Abraham Lincoln kept four cats in the White House. When his wife, Mary Todd Lincoln, was asked if he had any hobbies, she supposedly said, "Cats."

4.

Cats have 230 bones—24 more bones than humans!

5.

Along with camels and giraffes, cats are the only animals that walk by moving both their right feet, then both their left.

Read all of Kitty's adventures!

Kitty's Magic — Misty the Scared Kitten

Ella Moonheart

Kitty's Magic — Shadow the Lonely Cat

Ella Moonheart

Kitty's Magic — Ruby the Runaway Kitten

Ella Moonheart

Kitty's Magic — Star the Little Farm Cat

Ella Moonheart

Kitty's Magic — Frost and Snowdrop the Stray Kittens

Ella Moonheart

Kitty's Magic — Sooty the Birthday Cat

Ella Moonheart

Kitty's Magic — Scout the School Cat

Ella Moonheart

Kitty's Magic — Bobby the Show-Off Cat

Ella Moonheart

www.bloomsbury.com
Facebook: KidsBloomsbury
Twitter: BloomsburyKids

Unicorn Princesses BY EMILY BLISS

Welcome to an enchanted land ruled by unicorn princesses!

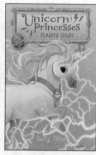

www.bloomsbury.com
Facebook: KidsBloomsbury
Twitter: BloomsburyKids

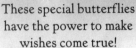

Don't miss Pippa's journey to find the golden horseshoes and save Chevalia!

Ella Moonheart grew up telling fun and exciting stories to anyone who would listen. Now that she's an author, she's thrilled to be able to tell stories to so many more children with her Kitty's Magic books. Ella loves animals, but cats most of all! She wishes she could turn into one just like Kitty, but she's happy to just play with her pet cat, Nibbles—when she's not writing her books, of course!